WHO ATE THE PIE?

Created by
Elio Villafranca

Illustrations by
Ute Zimmermann

AuthorHouse™
1663 Liberty Drive
Bloomington, IN 47403
www.authorhouse.com
Phone: 1 (833) 262-8899

Because of the dynamic nature of the Internet, any web addresses or links contained in this book may have changed since publication and may no longer be valid. The views expressed in this work are solely those of the author and do not necessarily reflect the views of the publisher, and the publisher hereby disclaims any responsibility for them.

Any people depicted in stock imagery provided by Getty Images are models, and such images are being used for illustrative purposes only. Certain stock imagery © Getty Images.

This book is printed on acid-free paper.

ISBN: 978-1-6655-0061-6 (sc)
ISBN: 978-1-6655-0062-3 (e)

Print information available on the last page.

Published by AuthorHouse 10/14/2020

author**HOUSE**®

WHO ATE THE PIE?

Created by Elio Villafranca

Illustrations by Ute Zimmermann

On a sunny Saturday afternoon, Mr. Goose heard that his friends were planning a party to celebrate the nice weather. Mr. Goose wanted to impress his animal friends, so he baked and baked, and made a deliciously beautiful apple pie to bring to the event.

Once the pie was ready, Mr. Goose pulled the hot pie out of the oven and placed it on the windowsill so it would cool off. He stepped out for a few minutes, only to find, upon his return, that...

"Oh No!" he flapped his wings! Alarmed, but not sad, Mr. Goose decided to investigate which one of his friends had eaten his delicious pie. He waddled to the back of his house and noticed that there were fresh footprints in the dirt under the window that did not look like his print.

"Aha!" he squawked. "It was not a goose that had come to the window and eaten my pie," he reasoned. But who was it?

Then Mr. Goose thought of a plan...

If I can find the match for these footprints, he said to himself, I will figure out who ate my pie.

Then Mr. Goose left the house in a hurry and started his quest.

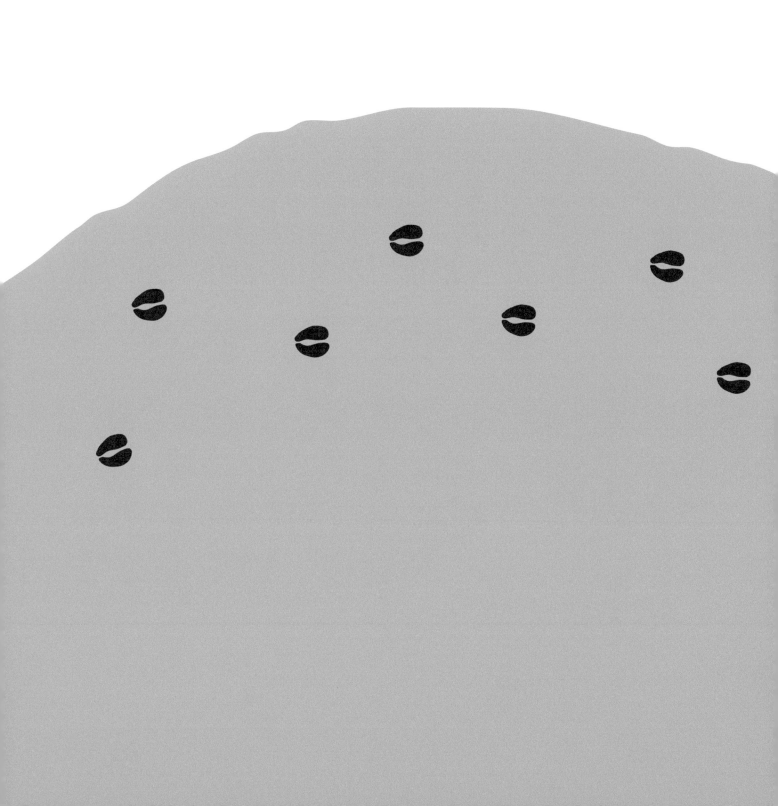

Mama Bear, Mama Bear,
Did you eat the pie that was there?

The Bear answered: **Growl, Growl**

Oh no my friend Goose, she said
This print does not match my foot.

Ask the Frog...

Mr. Frog, Mr. Frog,
Did you hide the pie under the log?

The Frog answered: **Croak, Croak**

Oh no my friend Goose, he said
This print does not match my foot.

Ask the Horse...

Bouncy Horse, bouncy Horse
Did you eat the pie that was baking in the stove?

The Horse answered: **Neigh, Neigh**

Oh no my friend Goose, he said
This print does not match my foot.

Ask the Cat...

Curious Cat, curious Cat,
Did you eat the pie and then take a nap?

The Cat answered: **Mew, Mew**

Oh no my friend Goose, he said
This print does not match my foot.

Ask the Duck…

Dear Duck, dear Duck,
Did you eat the pie as you walked?

The Duck answered: **Quack, Quack**

Oh no my friend Goose, she said
This print does not match my foot.
Ask the Hippo…

Señor Hippo, Señor Hippo
Did you eat the pie, as you walked
on your tiptoe?

The Hippo answered:
Grunt, Groan, Growl,
Roar, Wheeze, Chuff

Oh no my friend Goose, he said
This print does not match my foot.

Ask the Penguin…

Mr. Penguin, Mr. Penguin,
Did you hide the pie
under your side-wing?

The Penguin answered: **Ehh, Ehh**

Oh no my friend Goose, he said
This print does not match my foot.

Ask the Pig…

Dear Pig, dear Pig
Did you eat the pie? Your belly is big.

The Pig answered: **Snort, Snort**

Oh no my friend Goose, he said
This print does not match my foot.

Ask the Chicken…

Dear Chicken, dear Chicken
Did you eat the pie that I baked this
weekend?

The Chicken answered: **Cluck, Cluck**

Oh no my friend Goose, she said
This print does not match my foot.

Ask the Dog...

Friendly Dog, friendly Dog
Did you eat the pie and then went
for a jog?

The Dog answered: **Woof, Woof**

Oh no my friend Goose, he said
This print does not match my foot.

Ask the Kangaroo...

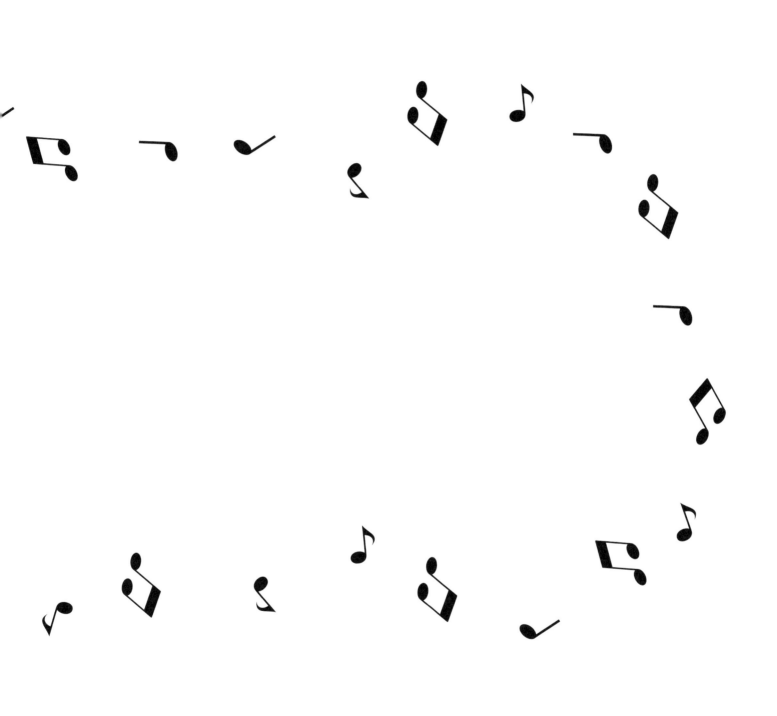

Dear Kangaroo, dear Kangaroo
Did you eat my pie? They said it was you.

The Kangaroo answered: **Chortle, Chortle**
Oh no my friend Goose, she said
This print does not
match my foot.

Ask the Cow…

Dear Cow, dear Cow,
How many slices did you eat and how?

Then the Cow rubbing her tummy said
Mmmm, Mmmm...

I wanted to taste one slice,
but it was so good that
I ate the entire pie!

 Penguin

 Cow

 Bear

 Cat

 Dog

 Duck

 Chicken

 Frog

 Hippo

 Horse

 Kangaroo

 Pig

The Baking Pie Song

Elio Villafranca

Printed in the United States
By Bookmasters